Published by Pleasant Company Publications
Based on the text by Katharine Holabird and the illustrations by Helen Craig
From the script by Diane Redmond

Visit our Web site at www.americangirl.com and
Angelina's very own site at www.angelinaballerina.com.

Book and necklace manufactured in China

05 06 07 08 09 10 C&C 10 9 8 7 6 5 4 3 2 1

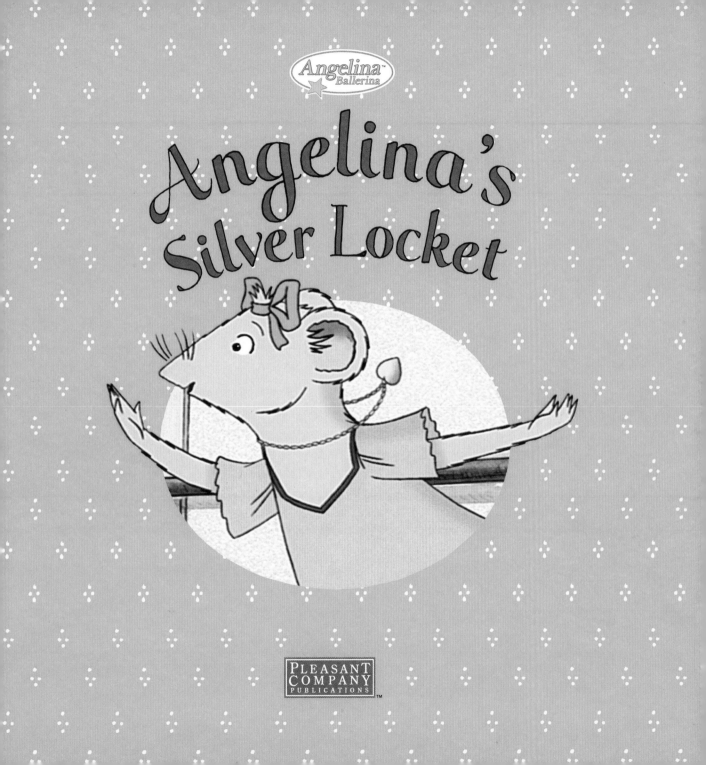

Angelina's Silver Locket

PLEASANT COMPANY PUBLICATIONS™

"I can't find my new hair ribbon," Angelina sighed, slumping over the kitchen table. "I need it for Miss Lilly's party!"

Beneath the table, little Polly played with something new of her own—a tiny purple purse, which she pushed along the floor in front of her.

"Let's get you ready for the party, Polly!" said
Mrs. Mouseling, scooping Polly up off the floor.

Angelina groaned. "Do I have to take her with me?"
she asked.

"I'm sure you'll both have a wonderful time," said
Mrs. Mouseling. "And your father and I need to get ready
for our dinner." The Mouselings were celebrating their
wedding anniversary with a special dinner out.

Angelina's best friend, Alice, arrived later that morning wearing a pretty green party dress and a string of colorful beads around her neck.

"Oh, Alice!" exclaimed Angelina. "You have a new necklace!"

Alice smiled proudly as she held up the polished beads. "My parents gave it to me," she said.

Angelina thought for a moment and then dashed down the hall to her mother's bedroom.

"Mum, may I borrow a necklace for the party?" Angelina asked eagerly.

But Mrs. Mouseling was going shopping. She was in such a rush that she didn't hear Angelina. "Have a lovely time, dear!" said Mrs. Mouseling as she hurried out the door.

Angelina saw that her mother had left her jewelry box open. Something sparkly caught Angelina's eye.

"Oh!" gasped Angelina as she lifted a shiny silver locket, shaped like a heart, from the velvet-lined box. It was perfect!

"The locket's very old," explained Angelina as Alice fastened the chain around Angelina's neck. "Dad gave it to Mum on their wedding day."

"How romantic!" sighed Alice. She peered around Angelina's shoulder. "Your mother *did* say you could borrow it, didn't she?"

Angelina swallowed hard. "Well . . . I tried asking her, but she was in a hurry," Angelina said softly. "Besides, she'll never know! I'll have it back before she gets home."

When Angelina, Alice, and Polly arrived at Miss Lilly's
Ballet School, the party was well under way. They nibbled
on snacks and visited with the Pinkpaws twins, who were
quite jealous of Angelina's silver locket.

"Our mother has a much prettier locket than that," sniffed Priscilla.

"Hers has a diamond in the middle," added Penelope.

"Well, this one is old and very precious," said Angelina, turning her back on the twins. "Come on, Alice, let's dance!"

As Angelina twirled around the room, the silver locket sparkled and swirled around her neck.

Miss Lilly helped Polly dance, too, by holding on to her little paws. "You're going to be a ballerina, just like your big sister," Miss Lilly said tenderly.

But Polly soon tired of the dancing and crawled away to explore the dance floor.

When the party finally came to an end, Angelina and Alice gathered their things and grabbed one last treat from the snack table. Angelina tucked Polly back into her pram.

Suddenly, Alice gasped. "Where's your silver locket?" she asked Angelina.

Angelina's hands flew to her neck. The locket was gone!

Angelina and Alice searched high and low for the silver
locket. Alice dropped to her knees and crawled beneath the
snack table, where she found nothing but trash and a few
cheesy crumbs.

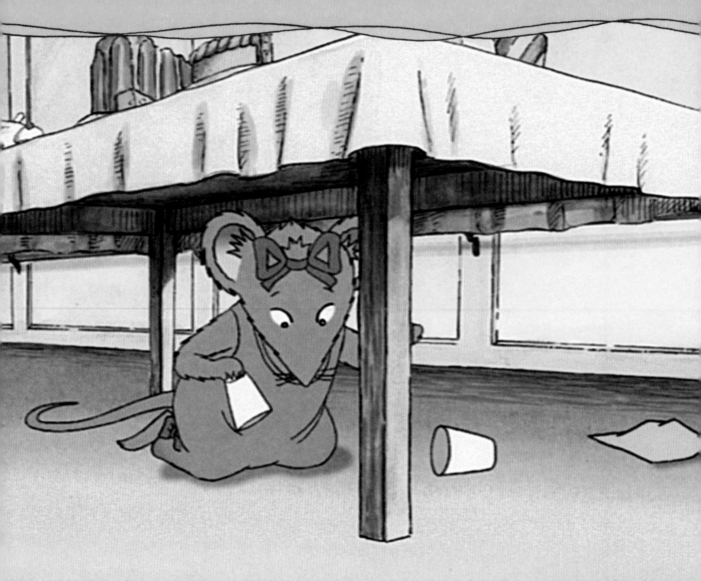

Angelina searched the dance floor and around the piano. "I've *got* to find it!" she cried. "What'll I say to Mum?"

"Don't worry, Angelina!" Alice called to her. "It must be here somewhere!"

As time passed, Angelina grew desperate. She climbed up and lifted the lid of the piano. "It might've fallen in here!" she said as tears began to well in her eyes. But the locket was nowhere to be found.

Angelina and Alice walked home slowly, pushing a tired, whimpering Polly in her pram. Angelina felt like crying, too. "I should never have borrowed the necklace," she whispered.

"I'm sure your mother won't be angry," Alice said kindly.

"Maybe not," sighed Angelina. She took a deep breath and then added hopefully, "Mum hardly ever wears the locket, so she might not even notice it's missing."

Just then, Mrs. Mouseling returned home with a big purple package. "Oh, Angelina!" she exclaimed. "I've bought the most beautiful dress to wear to dinner tonight. It'll go perfectly with the silver locket your father gave me!"

"I can't wait to see how the dress and the necklace will look together," said Mrs. Mouseling as she comforted little Polly. "Would you please bring me my jewelry box, Angelina?"

Angelina's heart thudded in her chest. She thought fast. "Oh . . . um . . . not right now," she stammered. "Polly's hungry. She needs you to feed her supper—right away!"

With that, Angelina dashed off down the lane, with Alice racing behind her.

At the jewelry store downtown, Angelina and Alice peered
through glass at dozens of beautiful necklaces. There were
lovely gold chains, strands of pearls, and pendants with
sparkling gemstones. But there were no lockets like
Mrs. Mouseling's.

"I don't know what to do, Alice," sniffled Angelina on the
bus ride home.

Alice tried to comfort her friend with a cheese roll. "Well . . .
if I'd lost something of yours," said Alice, "something very
precious, what would you want me to do?"

"I'd want you to tell me the truth," answered Angelina tearfully.

Alice nodded solemnly. "That's what you have to do, Angelina. You have to tell your mother the truth."

Back home, Angelina bravely pushed open the front door.
She found Mr. and Mrs. Mouseling frantically searching
the kitchen.

"It can't be lost," said Mr. Mouseling, bending over to look
beneath the kitchen table.

"I'm sure I saw it earlier," said Mrs. Mouseling as she
rummaged around near the windowsill.

Angelina took a deep breath. "You won't be able to find it!" she blurted out. "I borrowed it for Miss Lilly's party, and I lost it!"

"What are you talking about?" asked Mrs. Mouseling as she turned to face Angelina. There, dangling from Mrs. Mouseling's neck, was the silver locket.

"Your necklace!" gasped Angelina.

"It's the oddest thing," said Mrs. Mouseling. "It was with your new hair ribbon in Polly's little purse. I don't know how on earth she got hold of them!"

Polly looked up innocently from the floor below. Her purse was tipped on its side, its contents spilled out.

"Oh!" exclaimed Angelina. She giggled with relief.

"Now we just have to find your father's tie," said Mrs. Mouseling as she turned to open the cupboard door.

Angelina was tucked into bed when Mr. and Mrs. Mouseling returned home from their anniversary dinner. They stood in the doorway, gazing at their daughter.

"She's growing up so fast," whispered Mrs. Mouseling lovingly. "She really is old enough now to wear my silver locket, don't you think?"

Angelina overheard her mother and sat up quickly. "Oh, no!" she exclaimed. "It's far too precious!" Then the older—and wiser—Angelina settled back down to sleep.